The Rivers Under the Earth

by Thornton Wilder

This play became available through the research and editing of F.J. O'Neil, of manuscripts in the Thornton Wilder Collection at Yale University.

A Samuel French Acting Edition

FOUNDED 1830

SAMUELFRENCH.COM
SAMUELFRENCH-LONDON.CO.UK

FOR PRODUCTION ENQUIRIES

UNITED STATES AND CANADA
Info@SamuelFrench.com
1-866-598-8449

AMATEUR RIGHTS IN THE
UNITED KINGDOM
Plays@SamuelFrench-London.co.uk
020-7255-4302

Each title is subject to availability from Samuel French, depending upon country of performance. Please be aware that *THE RIVERS UNDER THE EARTH* may not be licensed by Samuel French in your territory. Producers should contact the nearest Samuel French office or licensing partner to verify availability.

For all enquiries regarding Professional productions in the United Kingdom; Professional and Amateur productions throughout the rest of Europe; and motion picture, television, and other media rights, please contact Alan Brodie Representation (Victoria@AlanBrodie.com). Visit www.thorntonwilder.com/contact for details.

No one shall make any changes in this title for the purpose of production. No part of this book may be reproduced, stored in a retrieval system, or transmitted in any form, by any means, now known or yet to be invented, including mechanical, electronic, photocopying, recording, videotaping, or otherwise, without the prior written permission of the publisher. No one shall upload this title, or part of this title, to any social media websites.

MUSIC USE NOTE

Licensees are solely responsible for obtaining formal written permission from copyright owners to use copyrighted music in the performance of this play and are strongly cautioned to do so. If no such permission is obtained by the licensee, then the licensee must use only original music that the licensee owns and controls. Licensees are solely responsible and liable for all music clearances and shall indemnify the copyright owners of the play and their licensing agent, Samuel French, against any costs, expenses, losses and liabilities arising from the use of music by licensees. Please contact the appropriate music licensing authority in your territory for the rights to any incidental music.

IMPORTANT BILLING AND CREDIT REQUIREMENTS

All producers of *THE RIVERS UNDER THE EARTH* must give credit to the author of the play in all programs distributed in connection with performances of the play, and in all instances in which the title of the play appears for the purposes of advertising, publicizing or otherwise exploiting the play and/or a production. The name of the author must appear on a separate line on which no other name appears, immediately following the title and must appear in size of type not less than fifty percent of the size of the title type.

This play may be performed only in its entirety. No permission can be granted for cuttings, readings or any use of parts of the play for any purpose whatsoever without the express written permission of the Wilder Family LLC. Absolutely *no* changes can be made to the text.

All producers of *THE RIVERS UNDER THE EARTH* must print the following credit 1/3 of the size of the author's name in the same boldness of type on the initial credits page of all programs distributed in connection with performances of the Play: "This/these [or title of play if more appropriate] became available through the research and editing of F.J. O'Neil."

FOREWORD TO
THE RIVERS UNDER THE EARTH
THE FOURTH PLAY IN THORNTON WILDER'S
AGES OF MAN ONE-ACT PLAY CYCLE

From the time he began dreaming up plays as a boy Thornton Wilder's vision of the theater transcended conventional boundaries, and to the end of his life his vision continually evolved and expanded. In 1956, he began work on what grew into an extravagantly ambitious project: two cycles of seven one-act plays based on the Deadly Sins and the Ages of Man. *The Rivers Under The Earth* is the fourth play in Wilder's series on the Ages of Man.

In what would prove to be his final dramatic works, Wilder sought not only to explore the theatrical possibilities inherent in the Sins and Ages, but (as he phrased it in his private journal on Christmas Day 1960) to "offer each play in the series as representing, also, a different mode of playwriting: Grand Guignol, Chekhov, Noh play, etc., etc." In short, he envisioned nothing less than a tour de force of dramatic theme and form encapsulated in the economy and intensity of the one-act play.

Wilder did not complete the challenge he set for himself, but he came close. The surviving work enriches his dramatic legacy and deserves to be remembered as more than a footnote to his lifelong conviction (written soon after *Our Town* opened on Broadway in 1938): "The theater offers to imaginative narration its highest possibilities."

THE SINS AND AGES THEN AND NOW

A brief overview of the history of these plays will help readers place them in Wilder's career as a dramatist. Two Sins, *Bernice* (Pride) and *The Wreck on the 5:25* (Sloth), premiered in English at a special event in Berlin in 1957 (with Wilder performing in *Bernice*). For reasons that have never been clear, for he enjoyed the experience and felt that plays did well, he withdrew them. That same year a third Sin, *The Drunken Sisters* (Gluttony), written as the satyr play for Wilder's full length drama, *The Alcestiad,* proved successful in its premiere on the stage of Zürich's fabled Schauspielhaus.

Five years passed before the continuation of his ambitious scheme appeared on a stage in the United States. In January 1962, two new Ages, *Infancy* and *Childhood,* and a new Sin, *Someone From Assisi* (Lust), opened at Circle in the Square, then located off-Broadway on Bleecker Street, to the reported largest pre-opening advanced sale in that stage's then 11-year history. Billed as "Plays for Bleecker Street," the show of ran for 349 performances.

Then silence. After "Plays for Bleecker Street" closed, no more Sins or Ages appeared. When Thornton Wilder died in 1975 the public record of his 14-play scheme contained only four plays – two Ages (*Infancy* and *Childhood*) and two Sins (Lust and Gluttony).

Today, eleven of Wilder's Sins and Ages are available for production: a completed cycle of the seven Deadly Sins and four of seven Ages of Man. The source of the seven "new" plays is no secret. The missing pieces were found in Thornton Wilder's archives at Yale[1]. From this source, starting in 1995, his literary executor and family released the two plays withdrawn in 1957, *Cement Hands* (Avarice), and four additional titles (*Youth, The Rivers Under the Earth* [Middle Age][2], *A Ringing of Doorbells* [Envy] and *In Shakespeare and the Bible* [Wrath]) recovered and completed by the actor, director and friend of Wilder's, F.J. O'Neil. (Mr. O'Neil's valuable notes on the origin of each of these missing links follow the text of each play.)

The public reception of Thornton Wilder's long lost and new plays was gratifying. *The Wreck on the 5:25* was selected as one of the Best American Short Plays of 1994-95. In 1997, the Centenary of the playwright's birth, Kevin Kline starred in a premiere reading in New York of *Cement Hands,* and the works recovered by Mr. O'Neil served as the centerpieces of Actors Theatre of Louisville's 13th Annual Brown-Forman Classics in Context Festival.   Finally, as the capstone to the Centenary celebration, TCG Press in 1997 published the 11 Sins and Ages in Volume I of *The Collected Short Plays of Thornton Wilder.*

---

[1] No additional one-acts remain to be discovered in Thornton Wilder's archives at Yale.

[2] We believe Wilder intended Rivers Under the Earth to represent Middle Age.

Wilder never followed conventional theatrical practice. As a young writer in his "Classic One Act Plays" of 1931, he swept away scenery and played provocative games with time and place. In the Sins and Ages, his farewell as a playwright, he is no less adventurous by way of settings, techniques, stage-craft and themes. One artistic trend of the day especially "fired his imagination" where these plays are concerned: his passionate belief in the value of the arena stage. "The boxed set play," he wrote in 1961, "encourages the anecdote…The unencumbered stage encourages the truth in everyone." Wilder felt so strongly that audiences should be seated as close to the actors as possible that Samuel French, for several years, was only permitted to license these plays to companies agreeing to perform them on a three-sided thrust or arena stage.

***

As part of its celebration of Wilder's one-act plays, Samuel French and the Wilder family take great pleasure in issuing new acting editions for the Sins and Ages long in print and, for the first time, acting editions of the seven new Wilder works. We invite those performing or teaching these plays to visit www.thorntonwilder.com for additional information.

– *Tappan Wilder,*
Literary Executor for Thornton Wilder

CHARACTERS

MRS. CARTER, mother, thirty-eight
TOM, her son, sixteen
FRANCESCA, her daughter, seventeen
MR. CARTER, their father, forty-three

SETTING

A few years ago. A point of land near a lake in southern Wisconsin.

*(At both sides of the stage are boxes of various sites, but none very large – orange boxes, canned goods boxes, covered with burlap or bits of rug. These are rocks. The action of this play takes place in the dark, but I wish it to be played in bright light. **MRS. CARTER**, very attractive and looking less than her thirty-eight years, enters tentatively feeling her way in the dark. She is followed by her son, **TOM**, sixteen.)*

MRS. CARTER. Take my hand, Tom. I don't know where you children inherited your ability to see in the dark.

*(**TOM** passes her and starts slowly leading her forward.)*

TOM. It isn't dark at all. All these stars reflected in the lake. – There's a sort of path here, Mother. The rocks are at the side of it.

MRS. CARTER. *(stopping)* Fireflies. All those fireflies. *(pause)* I don't know why it is that when I see fireflies I think of *horses* – no, of an old horse named Billy that we used to have when we were children.

TOM. Fireflies – and a horse!!

MRS. CARTER. *(still standing and smiling)* There are many associations like that one can't explain. – Why does your father dislike the color green? Why do I always make a mistake when I add a six and a seven? Why have I an ever so faint tiny prejudice against people whose name begins with B-Blodgetts and Burnses and Binghams and even dear old Mrs. Becket.

*(**TOM** leads her a step forward.)*

TOM. I haven't got any quirks like that.

MRS. CARTER. *(stopping again)* Why have we never been able to make you eat rice?

TOM. Ugh! – I just don't like it!

MRS. CARTER. Why does your sister hate to sit in the back-seat of automobiles?

TOM. Oh, Francesca's crazy, anyway.

MRS. CARTER. Oh, no she isn't. She's the most reasonable and logical of us all.

TOM. Why does Francesca hate to come here?

MRS. CARTER. What?

TOM. She hates to come out on this point of land. She told me once – but then she was sorry she told me. She told me that every now and then she dreamed that she was on this point of land, and that when she dreamed it, it was a nightmare and she woke up crying or screaming or something.

MRS. CARTER. *(thoughtful)* You mustn't tease her about it. Promise me you won't tease her about it.

TOM. All right.

MRS. CARTER. Now take my elbow and lead me to a rock that I can remember at the very tip of the point. *(as they progress)* No – all those quirks, as you call them, are like wrecks at the bottom of the sea. They mark the place where there was once a naval battle – or a storm. Why did my dear father always become angry whenever anybody mentioned… – Thank you, Tom. Here it is! I used to come and sit here when I was a girl. There aren't any snakes are there?

TOM. *(competent)* One: snakes don't like this kind of pine needles; two: snakes in America don't come out at night.

MRS. CARTER. You're such a pleasure, Tom; you know everything. What I mean is: you know everything comforting. – Now you go back and do whatever it is you were doing.

(**TOM** *stands irresolute in the middle of the stage, looking up.*)

TOM. When do you want me to come and lead you back?

MRS. CARTER. Forget me, Tom. I can find my way back now.

(Girl's voice off: "T-o-o-m!...Tom C-a-a-arter.")

TOM. *(warningly, to his mother)* Hsh!

(The voice, passing in the distance: "T-o-o-m!")

TOM. Polly Springer's always wanting something. Golly, those girls are helpless. They can't even stick a marshmallow on a fork...The moon will rise over *there*...You came to this very place?

MRS. CARTER. In those days we knew everyone in all the houses around the lake. Many times I'd come and spend the night with the Wilsons...or the Kimballs. *(She indicates first the right, then the left.)* And I'd slip away from them, and come here; and think...We were told that this point had been some sort of Indian ceremonial campground...and a burial place, I suppose. Your father used to find arrowheads here.

TOM. What did you used to think about?

MRS. CARTER. Oh, what do young girls think about?...I remember once...I made a vow: never to marry. Yes. I was going to be a doctor. And at the same time I was going to be a singer. But I wasn't going to sing in concerts...for money. I was going to sing to my patients in the wards just before they turned out the lights for the night. That's the kind of thing young girls think about.

*(**TOM** has been taking this in very gravely, his eyes on the distance. He says abruptly.)*

TOM. But you *did* get married. And you almost never sing anymore. – I brought your guitar.

MRS. CARTER. What!?

TOM. Yes. I knew they'd ask you to sing later – around the bonfire.

MRS. CARTER. Why, Tom, you little devil. They would never have thought of it. Now don't you go putting the idea into their heads.

TOM. I didn't. I heard them talking about it. I canoed back across the lake and got your guitar...You don't *hate* to sing.

MRS. CARTER. Oh, I'll sing, if anybody asks me to. It's not important enough to make any discussion about.

(Silence. TOM lies down in the path facing the sky, his head on his folded arms.)

TOM. Right up there…in the Milky Way…There's something called a Coal Hole.

MRS. CARTER. What?

TOM. A Coal Hole. It's sort of a deep empty stocking. If Father gave me a Jaguar; and I started driving five thousand miles a minute – *starting* from up there – it'd take me hundreds of millions of years to get halfway through it. – Lake water has a completely different sound of slapping – or lapping – than water at the seashore, hasn't it? I like it best.

(He shuts his eyes. Girls' voices, giggling and talking excitedly, are heard near the entrance. TOM sits up energetically and calls:)

TOM. Mildred! Constance! – Is that you, Constance?

VOICE. Ye-e-s!

TOM. Get me a hamburger! Be a sweetie!

VOICE. *(sweetly)* Get it yourself, deeeer bo-oo-y.

TOM. *(lying down again; darkly)* The slaves are getting uppish at the end of the summer.

MRS. CARTER. Would these be the same trees that were here twenty years ago?

TOM. Yes. Red pines grow fast the first five years, then they settle down and grow about a foot a year. *(He turns to lie on his stomach, leaning on his elbow. He explains simply and casually.)* This is really a sand dune here. Until recently there was a great big lake over all this area. When the lake shrunk, there were these dunes. Ordinarily, it takes about five thousand years for the first grasses to get their roots in and to make enough humus for small bushes to grow. Then it takes about 10,000 years for the bushes to make enough humus for the white pines. Then come the red pines. Probably it was faster here because of these rocks. They prevented the top sand from being blown away every few days. That's why the trees are so much bigger here, and over at the Cavanaughs, and around the boat club…Rocks.

FRANCESCA'S VOICE. *(off)* Mo-o-ther!

MRS. CARTER. Yes, dear, here I am.

*(Enter **FRANCESCA**, seventeen, with a scarf.)*

FRANCESCA. Father said you'd probably be here.

TOM. *(rolling to one side)* Don't step on me, you galoot!

FRANCESCA. Oh, you're here. – Goodness, a regular jungle. – Father said you're to put this shawl on. He's bringing a blanket.

MRS. CARTER. I'm too warm as it is. Well, give it to me. Thank you, dear.

FRANCESCA. What are you doing out here?

TOM. *(bitingly)* We're talking about you. *(imitating a teacher)* "I was just saying to Mrs. Carter I don't know what's to become of Francesca. In all my ninety years of teaching I've never known such a problem child."

FRANCESCA. *(airily; leaving)* Tz-tz-tz.

TOM. *(urgently)* Be a sweet little flower box and get me a hamburger.

FRANCESCA. Mother, don't you let Tom have another. Everybody's laughing at him. James Wilson says he had eight. – If you want to make a howling pig of yourself, you can just get up and fetch your own. *(leaning over him maliciously)* Of course, I don't know what Miss What's-Her-Name will think of you gorging yourself like that. – Mother, Tom has been making a perfect fool of himself over a new girl – a cousin of the Richardsons. Anybody can see she's a perfect nothing, but there's Tom: "Violet, you didn't get any peach ice cream. Violet…"

TOM. *(covering her speech)* Quack-quack-quack. Honk-honk-honk.

FRANCESCA. Violet this and Violet that. *(louder)* He even started a fight over her.

TOM. *(rising and starting off)* Quack-quack-quack! I'll be back. Honk-honk-honk.

(TOM leaves.)

MRS. CARTER. When you're by yourself, Francesca, you're of course much older than Tom. But when you're *with* Tom, you're younger – and *much* younger. I wish someone could explain that to me.

FRANCESCA. Well, as far as I'm concerned, he's been an eight-year-old for years. And always will be.

MRS. CARTER. To get to know the best of Tom, you must learn to *(She puts her hand on her lips.)* hold your tongue. It's always a pleasure to be silent with Tom. You try it someday.

FRANCESCA. Why should I hold my tongue with him?

MRS. CARTER. Have you noticed how your father holds his tongue with you?

FRANCESCA. I don't talk *all the time* when I'm with Father.

MRS. CARTER. No. But when you do, you talk so *well.*

FRANCESCA. *(softened; with wonder)* Do I? *(kneeling before her mother)* Do I, really?

MRS. CARTER. I shouldn't have to tell you that.

FRANCESCA. Thank you.

*(enter **MR. CARTER**, forty-three, lawyer, with a blanket)*

MR. CARTER. Mary?

MRS. CARTER. Here I am, Fred.

MR. CARTER. Try this rock. It's drier. *(He puts the blanket on a rock.)* Can you see?

MRS. CARTER. *(crossing)* Yes. – What's this about a fight Tom had?

FRANCESCA. He's in a terrible mood tonight. First, that fight with the MacDougal boy – I wasn't there. Just some craziness or other.

MRS. CARTER. Do you know anything about it, Fred?

MR. CARTER. Yes. I'll tell you about it later.

FRANCESCA. But that's not really what upset him. A very funny thing happened. Before supper we were all lying around the dock and somebody said that you were going to sing tonight at the bonfire. And that boy from Milwaukee said: "Mrs. Carter sing! *She's too old!*" (**FRANCESCA** *thinks this is very funny. Gales of laughter*) He'd mixed you up with Mrs. Cavanaugh!! And Paul or Herb said: "She isn't *old.* She isn't any older than…" their own mothers. And the boy from Milwaukee said: "Sure, she's old. She's nice and all that, but she oughtn't to be allowed to sing." He thought Mrs. Cavanaugh was *you*!! *(more laughter)* But you should have seen Tom's face!

MRS. CARTER. What?

FRANCESCA. Tom's face. You'd have thought he was seeing a ghost. And the boy from Milwaukee said: "Why, she's got all those gray hairs." *(gales of laughter)* You remember how at breakfast a few days ago you said you'd found some more gray hairs?

MRS. CARTER. Yes.

FRANCESCA. And Tom was *believing* all this was about you. Well, I thought he'd either…jump on the boy and kill him, or go away and…maybe throw up.

MR. CARTER. What did he do?

MRS. CARTER. He canoed back across the lake to get my guitar.

MR. CARTER. Francesca, I want to talk to your mother alone a moment.

FRANCESCA. *(touch of pique)* All right…but kindly don't… mention…*me.*

(She goes out; very queenly. Pause.)

MR. CARTER. Well, what do you think about that?…I suppose in the code, a boy can't strike another boy for calling his mother an old woman…Tom learns about old age.

MRS. CARTER. What was this other story about a fight?

MR. CARTER. Very odd. Very odd. Tom is not a bulldog type. There's a new girl here – a cousin of the Richardsons. I don't know her name.

MRS. CARTER. Violet.

MR. CARTER. Yes, Violet Richardson. It looks as though Tom had taken a sudden fancy to her. She doesn't seem interesting to me – neither pretty nor individual. Anyway, he was sitting beside her – and the MacDougal boy – the bigger one – Ben – came up and began pulling at her arm…to get her to go over where some of them were dancing. Suddenly Tom got up in an awful rage. Told him to let her alone. She was talking to him. Not to stick his nose in where he wasn't wanted. It all flared up in a second: two furious roosters; two stags fighting over a doe. The MacDougal boy backed down. I think he went home. It was all over in a second, too – but it was *real*…it was very real and hot.

(slight pause)

MRS. CARTER. And I thought this was going to be just one more dull picnic!

(**MR. CARTER** *lights a pipe and goes to sit on the rock where his wife had been sitting.*)

Fred, Tom just told me that Francesca hated to come *here* – that she had bad dreams about it? Did you ever know that?

MR. CARTER. What? – Here, this point of land!

MRS. CARTER. Can you think of any reason for it?

MR. CARTER. No!

MRS. CARTER. I'll give you a hint: a robin redbreast.

MR. CARTER. What are you getting at?

MRS. CARTER. A dead robin?…The children were about six and seven. We had told them there had been an Indian graveyard here. They had found a dead robin in the woods, and they set out to bury it…I came on such solemn hymn singing and preaching and praying… That night Francesca was deathly ill –

MR. CARTER. Do I remember!! It was one of the most shattering experiences in my life!!

MRS. CARTER. Dr. Macintosh kept asking us what she had eaten, and I – stupidly, stupidly – failed to connect convulsions and hysterics with the burial of Robin Red Breast. Francesca had learned about death… You sat soothing her and reading aloud to her until the sun rose.

MR. CARTER. And ever since she dislikes the color red.

MRS. CARTER. And the same experience had no effect on Tom, whatever. Yet we always think of Tom as the sensitive one and Francesca as the sensible one.

MR. CARTER. I guess, growing up is one long walk among perils – among yawning abysses… *(silence)* Well, since you're talking about old times – I'm going to interrogate you. We've just heard that Tom had a fight. A fight over a girl named Violet. Does the name Violet bring back anything to you?

MRS. CARTER. No…No, why?

MR. CARTER. The color?

MRS. CARTER. No.

MR. CARTER. Think a minute. *(she shakes her head)* A dress you wore?

MRS. CARTER. Fred, you wouldn't remember that! Your sister brought me back from Italy that beautiful silk. I had a dress made from it.

MR. CARTER. Go on.

MRS. CARTER. Then I bought various things to match it… beads…

MR. CARTER. I called it "your violet year"…perfume!…

MRS. CARTER. Absurd…just before the war…1940 and '41. *(pause)* What are you implying? Tom wouldn't have known anything about that!

MR. CARTER. *(dismissing it unhesitatingly)* Of course not. He would have been only two. *(with teasing, flirtatious intention)* It was *myself* I was thinking of. He is infatuated with a Violet, just as I was.

MRS. CARTER. Now, go away…to think wives wear…you're in the way, Fred.

MR. CARTER. *(with a low laugh)* Well, I've had my troubles on that rock, too.

(TOM appears at the entrance, carrying a guitar.)

TOM. I could have found my way here by the smell of Father's pipe. *(He stops, closes his eyes and smells it.)* Christmas is coming. You'll need some more of that tobacco. *(he gropes)* I know its name. No, don't help me…ah! "Bonny Prince Charlie."

(He puts the guitar on his mother's lap.)

MRS. CARTER. What's this? Oh – my guitar. Maybe they won't call for me.

MR. CARTER. *(starting off)* Are you sure you're warm enough? – Tom, do you remember coming out here with Francesca when you were six and holding a funeral over a robin redbreast?

TOM. *(lightly)* No, did I? Did I, really? – Why?

MRS. CARTER. We were just wondering, Tom.

(Exit MR. CARTER. TOM gets down on his knees preparatory to lying down again.)

TOM. I helped the squad that was picking up the trash. I rolled the ice cream cans to the truck. I showed Polly Springer how to put a marshmallow on a fork. – I've done my duty. I can rest. *(silence)* Mother, make one chord on the guitar.

(She does a slow arpeggiated chord. Silence.)

One note of music out of doors is worth ten thousand in a building. *(He again turns over on his stomach, raises himself on his elbows.)* Mother, I'm going to be the doctor that you planned to be.

MRS. CARTER. Oh! – Not an astronomer? Or a physicist?

TOM. No. That's all too far away. I'm going to be a research doctor.

MRS. CARTER. *(not hurrying)* Well, you don't have to decide now.

TOM. *(decisively)* I've decided. – Last month I thought maybe I'd be one of those new physicists. I'd find something that could stop every atomic bomb…I think others'll get there before me…Besides, that's not hard enough. Any Joe will be able to find that one of these days. I want something harder…something nearer. For instance –

(Voice offstage "MRS. CAAAR-TER." Nearer "MRS. CAAAR-TER!")

MRS. CARTER. *(raising her voice)* Ye-es. Here I am.

VOICE. The bonfire's starting. They want you to come and sing.

MRS. CARTER. Is that you, Gladys? Tell them to start singing. I'll come soon.

VOICE. All-riiight.

MRS. CARTER. You were saying you wanted to do something harder.

TOM. Harder and *nearer. (beating the ground)* There's no reason people have got to grow old so fast. I guess everybody's got to grow old some day. But I'll bet you we can discover lots of things that will put it off. I'll bet you that three hundred years from now people will think that we were just stupid about, well, about growing old so soon…I haven't any crazy idea about people living forever; but…it's funny: I don't mind getting old, but I don't like it to happen to other people. Anyway, that's decided. *(He puts his head in his arms and closes his eyes as though going to sleep.)* It's great to have something decided. *(pause)* Mother, what was the name of that nurse I had when I was real young, the southern one?

MRS. CARTER. Miss…Miss Forbes.

TOM. What was her first name?

MRS. CARTER. Let me think a minute…Maude? No. *(trouvé)* Madeleine!

TOM. Do you remember any teacher I had back then that was named…Violet?

MRS. CARTER. …N-n-n-o.

TOM. *(dreamily)* There must have been somebody…I remember…it was like floating…and the smell of violets. Golly, I go crazy when I smell them. I'll tell you why I was so polite to old Mrs. Morris – you remember? She had perfume of violets on her. Why don't you ever wear that, Mother? Don't you like it?

MRS. CARTER. *(caught)* Why, it…never occurred to me.

TOM. That's an idea for a Christmas present, maybe.

(Voices "MRS. CAAAR-TER!")

MRS. CARTER. Here they come.

*(Enter **MR. CARTER.**)*

MR. CARTER. Do you feel like singing or not? They're making a fuss about you down there.

MRS. CARTER. Why not?

*(Enter **FRANCESCA**, running.)*

FRANCESCA. Mother, they're stamping their feet and –

MRS. CARTER. I'm coming. – I… *(She starts tuning the guitar. Going out.)* What'll I do, Tom? I'll do…

(They are out. Silence.)

FRANCESCA. The fireflies…the moon.

*(**MR. CARTER** takes the blanket from the rock, carries it across the stage and wraps it around the rock he formerly sat on; then, sitting on the floor, leans his back against it.)*

FRANCESCA. *(cont.)* Your pipe smells so wonderful in the open air. *(she starts quietly laughing)* Papa, I'll tell you a secret. *Years* ago – when I went away to summer camp – do you know what I did? I went into your study, and I stole some of that tobacco. I put it in an envelope. And in the tent after lights out, I'd take it out and smell it…Why do they call it "Bonny Prince Charlie"? *(pause; dreamily)* I like the name of Charlie…I've never known a stupid boy named Charles. Isn't that funny? They all have something about them that's interesting. *(She starts laughing again.)* But I'll tell you something else: all Freds are terrible. Really terrible. You're the only Fred *(laughing and scarcely audible)* that I can *stand.*

MR. CARTER. Look at the moonlight just hitting the top of the boat club.

(She turns on her knees and draws in her breath, rapt.
MR. CARTER *drawing his fingers over the ground.)*

When I was a boy I found all sorts of things here. I made a collection and got a prize for it. Arrowheads and ax heads…I used to come out here and think – on this very rock.

FRANCESCA. *(glowing)* Did you? – What did you think *about?*

MR. CARTER. That someday maybe I'd have a family. That someday maybe I'd go into politics.

FRANCESCA. And now you're senator!

MR. CARTER. Tom's not interested in this place as a *human* place. He's always talking about it as a place before there were any human beings here. But even as boy, I used to think all that must have gone on here. – Initiations –

FRANCESCA. What?

MR. CARTER. Initiations into the tribe. And councils about those awful white skins. And buryings. *(pause)* On this very rock I decided to become a lawyer.

FRANCESCA. *(moving a few feet toward him on her knees)* Papa, why was I so mean to Mother?

MR. CARTER. Mean?

FRANCESCA. *(bent head, slowly)* Yes, I was. When I was telling that story about the boy from Milwaukee…mistaking Mother for an old woman, like Mrs. Cavanaugh. I knew I was mean while I was doing it. *(she sobs)* And why am I mean about Tom? I *am.* I *am. (sinking lower on her heels)* I'm terrible. I'm unforgivable. – But *why?*

MR. CARTER. Are you mean about yourself? *(She stares at him.)* Yes, now you're being mean toward yourself! – Could you imagine building a house on this point?

FRANCESCA. No...

MR. CARTER. Because you'd have to cut down so many trees?

FRANCESCA. *(slight pause)* No...I could do it without cutting down the best trees.

MR. CARTER. Why couldn't you imagine building here?

FRANCESCA. *(lightly)* I wouldn't.

MR. CARTER. No *reason?*

FRANCESCA. *(affectionately)* Why do you keep asking me when you can *see* that I don't want to answer.

MR. CARTER. Oh, I beg your pardon.

FRANCESCA. *(in a loud whisper)* I don't like this point. I've never liked it.

MR. CARTER. *(walking back and forth, right to left)* Well, isn't that funny – people feeling so differently about things.

*(**MR. CARTER** holds out his hand and **FRANCESCA** moves closer and takes his hand. They both look into the distance, lost in their thoughts and feelings, as the lights fade.)*

End of Play

A NOTE ON THE TEXT

The place of *The Rivers Under the Earth* in Wilder's schema of short plays is ambiguous. In its first draft it was entitled *Children*. That title was dropped in later drafts. Students of Wilder have speculated that he finally meant the play to represent middle age, since *Childhood* was the title given to one of the three "Plays for Bleecker Street," produced in 1962 at Circle in the Square in New York City.

Wilder had written in his journal[1] "I planned [Rivers] to arrive at a culmination illustrating – so recurrent in me – the relations between a daughter and a father." I added the final stage direction *(in brackets)* to illustrate this idea in a concluding tableau. The author's manuscript had ended with the line:

MR. CARTER. *(walking back and forth, right to left):* Well, isn't that funny – people feeling so differently about things.

F. J. O'Neil
April 1997

---

1. *The Journals of Thornton Wilder 1939-1961*, entry 749, page 265, selected and edited by Donald Gallup, Yale University Press, 1985.

THORNTON WILDER (1897-1975) was an accomplished novelist and playwright whose works explore the connection between the commonplace and the cosmic dimensions of human experience. He won three Pulitzer Prizes: for his novel *The Bridge of San Luis Rey*, and two plays, *Our Town* and *The Skin of Our Teeth*. Wilder's farce, *The Matchmaker*, was adapted as the musical *Hello, Dolly!* He also enjoyed enormous success as a translator, adaptor, actor, librettist and lecturer/teacher. Wilder's many honors include the Gold Medal for Fiction from the American Academy of Arts and Letters and the Presidential Medal of Freedom. Penelope Niven's definitive biography, *Thornton Wilder: A Life*, was published in October 2012. For more information, please visit www.thorntonwilder.com.

Also by
Thornton Wilder

The Beaux' Stratagem (with Ken Ludwig)
The Matchmaker
The Alcestiad
Our Town
The Skin of Our Teeth

<u>**Thornton Wilder One Act Series: The Ages of Man**</u>
Infancy
Childhood
Youth
The Rivers Under the Earth

<u>**Thornton Wilder One Act Series: The Seven Deadly Sins**</u>
The Drunken Sisters
Bernice
The Wreck on the 5:25
A Ringing of Doorbells
In Shakespeare and the Bible
Someone From Assisi
Cement Hands

<u>**Thornton Wilder One Act Series: Wilder's Classic One Acts**</u>
The Long Christmas Dinner
Queens of France
Pullman Car Hiawatha
Love and How to Cure It
Such Things Only Happen in Books
The Happy Journey to Trenton and Camden

www.thorntonwilder.com